GRANDPARENTS'

J O U R N A L

Mother and Son, Egon Schiele

MUSEUM OF FINE ARTS, BOSTON
UNIVERSE GRAPHICS, NEW YORK

Front Cover Illustration:

Charles Hopkinson
(American)
The Hopkinson Family Portrait (detail), 1923
Oil on canvas, 51 ½ x 64 ½ inches
Gift of Mrs. J.H. Barr, Mrs. Isabella Halsted,
Mrs. Alfred Rive, Mrs. William A. Shurcliff,
and Mrs. Lovell Thompson, daughters of
Charles Hopkinson
1980.661

First Published in the United States of America in 1993
by Universe Publishing
300 Park Avenue South
New York, NY 10010

Project coordinators: Kathyrn Sky-Peck and Susan Carpenter
Designed by Christina Bliss

ISBN 1-55550-869-3

Printed and bound in Hong Kong

GREAT GRAND

GREAT GREAT GRAND

MOTHER

FATHER

MOTHER

FATHER

MOTHER

FATHER

MOTHER

FATHER

MOTHER

FATHER

MOTHER

FATHER

MOTHER

FATHER

MOTHER

FATHER

MOTHER

FATHER

MOTHER

FATHER

MOTHER

FATHER

CONTENTS

LITTLE THINGS

Little drops of water,
Little grains of sand,
Make the mighty ocean
And the beauteous land.

And the little moments,
Humble though they be,
Make the mighty ages
Of eternity.

So our little errors
Lead the soul away,
From the paths of virtue
Into sin to stray.

Little decks of kindness,
Little words of love,
Make our earth an Eden,
Like the heaven above.

Julie A. Carney

Hymns and Sacred Songs, 1855

THE FIRST
GRANDCHILD

Mother and Child, Marie Danforth Page

Mother and Child, George de Forest Brush

"To Walter Jr.," from *Rhymes of Real Children*, Jessie Wilcox Smith

THE
GRANDCHILD

Jacques Bergeret as a Child, Pierre Auguste Renoir

Calm Morning, Frank Weston Benson

THE
GRANDCHILD

Little Agnes, Laura Coombs Hills

Writing to Father, Jonathan Eastman Johnson

"Mother and Child," from *Rhymes of Real Children*,
Jessie Wilcox Smith

THE ――――
GRANDCHILD

Helen Carpenter (née Shepherd) at Age 5, Maria Judson Strean

2 3

The Daughters of Edward D. Boit, John Singer Sargent

CEREMONIAL
CELEBRATIONS

Emma and Her Children, George Wesley Bellows

BIRTHDAYS

Under the Horse Chestnut Tree, Mary Cassatt

Cover from *Rhymes of Real Children*, Jessie Wilcox Smith

Edward Everett Hale 3rd, Laura Coombs Hills

SUMMER
OUTINGS

Summer at Campobello, New Brunswick, Edward Wilbur Dean Hamilton

Carnival (Franklin Park, Boston), Maurice Prendergast

FAMILY
HOLIDAYS

The Hopkinson Family Portrait, Charles Hopkinson

Charlotte Nichols Greene and her Son Stephen, John Singer Sargent

The Tea Party, Henry Sargent

The Artist's Daughter Asleep (facing left), Jean-Michel Moreau

THE GRANDCHILDREN COME TO
VISIT

Camille Monet and a Child in the Artist's Garden in Argenteuil, Oscar Claude Monet

GRANDCHILDREN'S
ACHIEVEMENTS

The Little Reader, Robert Walter Weir

The Little Convalescent, Jonathan Eastman Johnson

Gathering Fruit, Mary Cassatt

ADVICE FROM
GRANDMOTHER

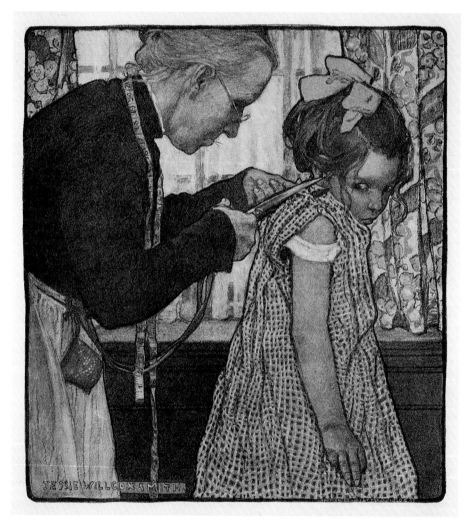

"Miss Mariar," from *Rhymes of Real Children*, Jessie Wilcox Smith

Double Portrait of Trudl, Oskar Kokoschka

ADVICE FROM
GRANDFATHER

John La Farge, Wilton Robert Lockwood

Robert de Cévrieux, John Singer Sargent

PHOTOGRAPHS

PHOTOGRAPHS

PHOTOGRAPHS

INDEX OF ILLUSTRATIONS

George Wesley Bellows
(American, 1882–1925)
Emma and Her Children, 1923
Oil on canvas, 59 x 65 inches
Gift of Subscribers and John
Lowell Gardner Fund
25.105

Frank Weston Benson
(American, 1862–1951)
Calm Morning, 1904
Oil on canvas, 44 x 36 inches
Gift of the Charles A.
Coolidge Family
1985.925

George de Forest Brush
(American, 1855–1941)
Mother and Child, 1895
Oil on circular panel,
38 ½ x 38 ½ inches
William Wilkins Warren
Collection Fund
95.1375

Mary Cassatt
(American, 1844–1926)
Gathering Fruit, about 1893
Drypoint, softground etching
and aquatint in color
16 ⅝ x 11 ¾ inches
Gift of William Emerson and
Charles Henry Hayden Fund
41.813

Under the Horse Chestnut Tree,
1896–97
Drypoint and aquatint in color
15 ⅞ x 11 ¼ inches
Bequest of W.G. Russell Allen
63.313

Edward Wilbur Dean Hamilton
(American, 1864–1943)
*Summer at Campobello, New
Brunswick*, about 1890–1900
Oil on canvas, 28 x 28 inches
Bequest of Maxim Karolik
64.463

Laura Coombs Hills
(American, 1859–1952)
Edward Everett Hale 3rd, 1915
Watercolor on ivory,
3 ½ x 2 ½ inches
Gift of Laura Coombs Hills
51.1935

Little Agnes (Agnes Mackintosh),
1911
Watercolor on ivory,
6 x 4 ½ inches
Gift of Laura Coombs Hills
51.1934

Charles Hopkinson
(American)
The Hopkinson Family Portrait,
1923
Oil on canvas, 51 ½ x 64 ½ inches
Gift of Mrs. J.H. Barr, Mrs.
Isabella Halsted, Mrs. Alfred
Rive, Mrs. William A. Shurcliff,
and Mrs. Lovell Thompson,
daughters of Charles Hopkinson
1980.661

Jonathan Eastman Johnson
(American, 1824–1906)
The Little Convalescent, about
1873–1879
Oil on academy board,
12 ¾ x 11 inches
Frederick Brown Fund
40.90

Writing to Father, 1863
Oil on canvas,
12 x 9 ½ inches
Bequest of Maxim Karolik
64.435

Oskar Kokoschka
(Austrian, 1886–1980)
Double Portrait of Trudl, 1931
Oil on canvas,
39 ¾ x 28 ⅛ inches
Seth K. Sweetser Fund
61.1138

Wilton Robert Lockwood
(American, 1861–1914)
John La Farge, 1891
Oil on canvas,
38 x 30 inches
Charles Henry Hayden Fund
09.208

Oscar Claude Monet
(French, 1840–1926)
*Camille Monet and a
Child in the Artist's Garden
in Argenteuil*, 1875
Oil on canvas,
21 ¾ x 25 ½ inches
Anonymous Gift in Memory of
Mr. and Mrs. Edwin S. Webster
1976.833

Jean-Michel Moreau
(French, 1741–1814)
*The Artist's Daughter Asleep
(facing left)*
Pen, black ink and wash,
4 x 5 15/16 inches
Bequest of Forsyth Wickes,
Forsyth Wickes Collection
65.2593

Marie Danforth Page
(American, 1869–1940)
Mother and Child, about 1910
Oil on canvas,
45 1/4 x 34 1/4 inches
Gift of Erville Maynard
1980.262

Maurice Prendergast
(American, 1858–1924)
Carnival (Franklin Park, Boston),
1897
Watercolor, 13 3/8 x 14 3/4 inches
Gift of the estate of
Nellie P. Carter
35.1689

Pierre Auguste Renoir
(French, 1841–1919)
Jacques Bergeret as a Child
Oil on canvas,
16 1/8 x 12 5/8 inches
Bequest of John T. Spaulding
48.595

Henry Sargent
(American, 1770–1845)
The Tea Party, 1879
Oil on canvas,
64 1/4 x 52 1/4 inches
Gift of Mrs. Horatio A. Lamb
in memory of Mr. and Mrs.
Winthrop Sargent
19.12

John Singer Sargent
(American, 1856–1925)
*Charlotte Nichols Greene and her
Son Stephen*, 1924
Charcoal on cream laid paper,
17 1/2 x 23 3/4 inches
Gift of Mrs. Stephen Greene
1986.970

*The Daughters of
Edward D. Boit*, 1882
Oil on canvas,
87 x 87 inches
Gift of Mary Louisa Boit,
Florence D. Boit, Jane Hubbard
Boit, and Julia Overing Boit,
in memory of their father,
Edward Darley Boit
19.124

Robert de Cévrieux, 1879
Oil on canvas, 33 1/2 x 19 1/4 inches
The Hayden Collection
22.372

Egon Schiele
(Austrian, 1890–1918)
Mother and Son, 1915
Charcoal and watercolor
19 x 12 1/2 inches
Edwin E. Jack Fund

Jessie Wilcox Smith
(American, 1863–1935)
"Miss Mariar," from *Rhymes
of Real Children*
(New York, 1913)
Color relief, 8 1/2 x 7 3/4 inches
Anonymous Gift

"Mother and Child," from
Rhymes of Real Children
(New York, 1913)
Color relief, 8 1/2 x 7 3/4 inches
Anonymous Gift

"To Walter Jr.," from *Rhymes
of Real Children*
(New York, 1913)
Color relief, 8 1/2 x 7 3/4 inches
Anonymous Gift

Cover from *Rhymes of Real
Children*
(New York, 1913)
Color relief, 8 1/2 x 7 3/4 inches
Anonymous Gift

Maria Judson Strean
(American, ?–1949)
*Helen Carpenter (née Shepherd)
at Age 5*
Watercolor on ivory,
3 5/8 x 2 3/4 inches
Gift of Mrs. Helen Carpenter
69.60

Robert Walter Weir
(American 1803–89)
The Little Reader
Watercolor, 7 3/8 x 6 1/2 inches
Gift of Maxim Karolik
57.296

GRANDMOTHER'S
FAMILY TREE

GRAND

_____
MOTHER

_____
MOTHER

_____
FATHER

_____
MOTHER

_____
FATHER

_____
FATHER

SEE INSIDE

BACK COVER FOR

GRANDFATHER'S

FAMILY TREE